W9-COY-021

WARNING!

Scaredy Squirrel insists you check your zippers before reading this book.

For Val and Dan  and for John, my dad

Copyright © 2021 by Melanie Watt

All rights reserved. Published in the United States by Random House Children's Books, a division of Penguin Random House LLC, New York. Published simultaneously in Canada by Tundra Books, Toronto, in 2021.

Random House and the colophon are registered trademarks of Penguin Random House LLC.

Visit us on the Web! rhcbooks.com

Educators and librarians, for a variety of teaching tools, visit us at RHTeachersLibrarians.com

Library of Congress Cataloging-in-Publication Data is available upon request.
ISBN 978-0-593-42896-2 (hardcover) — ISBN 978-0-593-30746-5 (pbk.)
ISBN 978-0-593-30747-2 (lib. bdg.) — ISBN 978-0-593-30748-9 (ebook)

MANUFACTURED IN CHINA
10 9 8 7 6 5 4 3 2 1
First Edition

Random House Children's Books supports the First Amendment and celebrates the right to read.

Penguin Random House LLC supports copyright. Copyright fuels creativity, encourages diverse voices, promotes free speech, and creates a vibrant culture. Thank you for buying an authorized edition of this book and for complying with copyright laws by not reproducing, scanning, or distributing any part in any form without permission. You are supporting writers and allowing Penguin Random House to publish books for every reader.

Melanie Watt

Scaredy Squirrel

Goes Camping

Random House New York

Scaredy Squirrel never goes camping. He'd rather be comfortable inside than risk going out in the rugged wilderness. Besides, setting up camp seems like a lot of trouble.

A few troublemakers Scaredy Squirrel is afraid could get too close for comfort:

skunks

mosquitoes

quicksand

the Three Bears

penguins

zippers

So he's found a simple way to sit back and enjoy camping from a safe distance.

Scaredy Squirrel sets up his new television. But he realizes there's a problem. He needs to plug it in.

Reaching the nearest electrical outlet will require major survival skills.

A few survival supplies Scaredy Squirrel needs to pack:

really long extension cord	Popsicles	tomato juice	bag of cemer

dictionary	pliers	instant oatmeal	fan

THE WILDERNESS OUTFIT

Netted hat
to dodge bugs

Penny
to bring good luck

Nose plug
to bypass nasty odors

Neckerchief
to scout

Water wings
to stay afloat

Badge
to signal peaceful intentions

Walkie-talkie
to stay in contact

Camouflage jacket
to blend into the great outdoors

Rubber boots
to be quick and dry

THE SCAREDY MOTTO: A prepared camper is a happy camper!

0530 HOURS:
Leave comfort zone.

0531 HOURS:
Run through woods.
Keep a low profile.

0541 HOURS:
Enter campground.

0545 HOURS:
Locate electricity.

0548 HOURS:
Plug in extension cord.

0549 HOURS:
Run back to home base.

0549 HOURS:
Get comfy and watch
The Joy of Camping.

SYMBOLS

Tent area

Play area

RV area

Washrooms

Trash area

Electrical
outlet

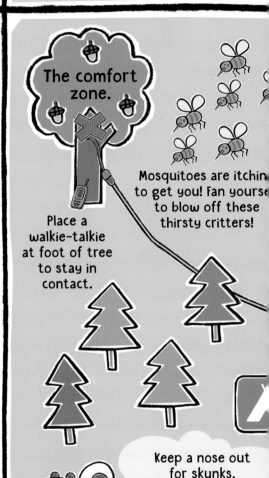

The comfort zone.

Place a walkie-talkie at foot of tree to stay in contact.

Mosquitoes are itchin to get you! Fan yourse to blow off these thirsty critters!

Keep a nose out for skunks. If sprayed, wash off the stink with gallons of tomato juice.

THE CAMPGROUND MISSION

Quicksand will bring you down! To avoid that sinking feeling, mix in cement.

You're not out of the woods until you get past the Three Bears. Their weakness — oatmeal! Serve them a quick bowl and do not snooze!

Campsites host a zillion zippers! If you get caught, use pliers to break loose!

Wherever there are coolers, penguins rule. They're as cold as ice and won't warm up to you! Toss Popsicles to occupy their sharp beaks.

Wear water wings to stay above it all.

Nose plugs are a must in this area!

Electrical outlet is here.

Note to self: If outlet is too high, use dictionary as step.

THE SCAREDY PLEDGE: Planning is everything!

THE RUBBER BOOT CAMP

WARM-UP ROUTINE:
(Repeat 143 times)

1.
2.
3.
4.

THE SCAREDY PROMISE: A fit squirrel is a safe squirrel!

AND FITNESS TRAINING CHART

OBSTACLE COURSE PRACTICE RUN:

THE SCAREDY LAW (of the fittest): Run, but never run into trouble!

THE OUTDOOR CONDITIONS

	GO	WAIT	CANCEL
☀️ SUN	☑	☐	☐
☁️ CLOUD	☐	☑	☐
🌧️ RAIN	☐	☑	☐
🌬️ WIND	☐	☑	☐
❄️ SNOW	☐	☑	☐
🌋 VOLCANO ACTIVITY	☐	☐	☑

THE SCAREDY RULE: If all else fails, take cover and play dead!

The following afternoon, right on schedule, Scaredy Squirrel proceeds toward the campground.

Scaredy tugs.

He pulls.

He loop-

the-loops.

But suddenly . . .

He bolts.

FORE!

He crashes.

He climbs.

He splashes.

He takes cover
and . . .

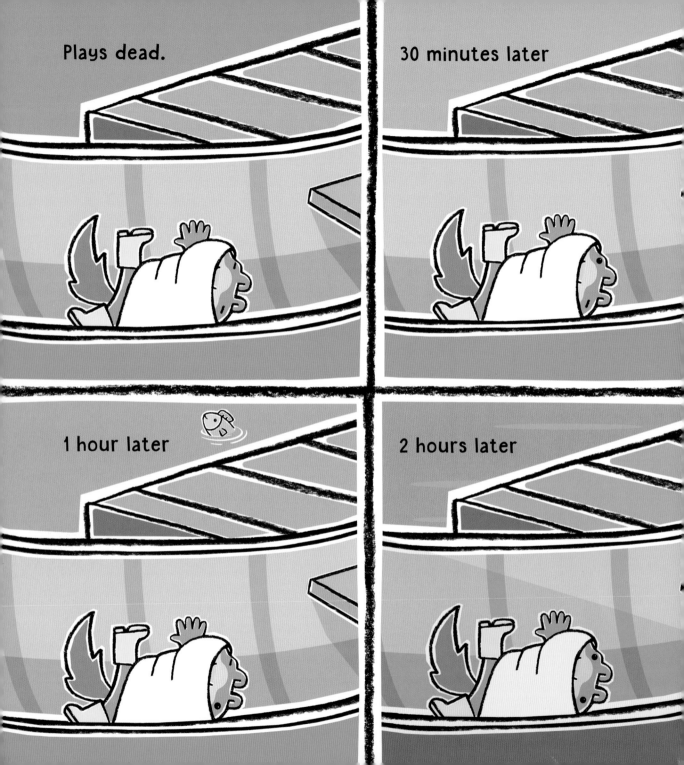

Scaredy Squirrel finally gets the drift.
He forgets all about the skunks, mosquitoes,
quicksand, Three Bears, penguins and zippers.

The wilderness isn't meant to be seen
from afar. It's meant to be enjoyed up close!

Scaredy breathes the fresh air . . .

savors roasted marshmallows . . .

gazes up
at the stars ...

gathers
pine cones ...

listens to songs ...
and gets comfortable.

Early the next morning, Scaredy Squirrel plugs in his extension cord and follows it back home.

This wild adventure
has inspired him to
approach camping
differently.

TOASTER

P.S. Some things are
worth the trouble.